Jamie
& Bubbie

A Book About People's Pronouns

Afsaneh Moradian

Illustrated by Maria Bogade

free spirit
PUBLISHING®

Library of Congress Cataloging-in-Publication Data
Names: Moradian, Afsaneh, author. | Bogade, Maria, illustrator.
Title: Jamie and Bubbie : a book about people's pronouns / Afsaneh Moradian; illustrated by Maria Bogade.
Description: Minneapolis, MN : Free Spirit Publishing Inc., 2020. | Audience: Ages 4–8.
Identifiers: LCCN 2020008138 (print) | LCCN 2020008139 (ebook) | ISBN 9781631985430 (hardcover) | ISBN 9781631985447 (pdf) |
    ISBN 9781631985454 (epub)
Subjects: CYAC: Gender identity—Fiction. | English language—Pronoun—Fiction. | Great-grandmothers—Fiction.
Classification: LCC PZ7.1.M66825 Jag 2020 (print) | LCC PZ7.1.M66825 (ebook) | DDC [E]—dc23
LC record available at https://lccn.loc.gov/2020008138
LC ebook record available at https://lccn.loc.gov/2020008139

Reading Level Grade 2; Interest Level Ages 4–8
Fountas & Pinnell Guided Reading Level M

Edited by Cassandra Sitzman
Cover and interior design by Shannon Pourciau

10 9 8 7 6 5 4 3 2 1
Printed in China
R18860720

Free Spirit Publishing Inc.
6325 Sandburg Road, Suite 100
Minneapolis, MN 55427-3674
(612) 338-2068
help4kids@freespirit.com
freespirit.com

FSC
www.fsc.org
MIX
Paper from responsible sources
FSC® C144853

For my grandmother

Jamie was excited.

Great Grandma Bubbie was coming for a visit.

They always had fun adventures.
Jamie couldn't wait.

Finally, Bubbie arrived. Jamie ran out to greet her.

"What are we doing today?" Jamie asked.

"It's such a lovely day. Let's take a walk," said Bubbie.

Jamie enjoyed seeing the neighbors outside and picking up fallen leaves.

Suddenly, Bubbie called, "Sir, you dropped your wallet! Jamie, be a dear and give that man his wallet."

Jamie loved to help. Running fast, Jamie reached
the person and tapped their arm.

Ms. Wallace turned and saw Jamie with her wallet.
"Thank you so much, Jamie!" said Ms. Wallace.

"You're welcome," Jamie said, and waved goodbye.

"Was he happy to get his wallet back?" Bubbie asked.

"Yes," said Jamie, "but that wasn't a man. That was Ms. Wallace. She lives in that yellow house."

"Is that so?" said Bubbie.

They walked around the corner, and Jamie said hi to some friends playing outside. Then Bubbie stopped to admire the rose bushes Mr. Anderson was watering. She and Jamie counted the roses.

Bubbie told Jamie and Mr. Anderson about the roses she planted when Jamie's mommy was little and how their dog would try to eat the flowers.

Soon it was lunchtime. Bubbie suggested stopping for pizza. "We don't have any napkins. Jamie, would you ask that woman if she'll give you some?"

"Bubbie, that person is a man," Jamie said.

"Oh, I'm sorry. I just assumed that was a woman."

After lunch Jamie and Bubbie stopped to look
in a bakery window.

"Hello, Mrs. Green!" said a young woman coming out
of the store. "Your friend Norma is my grandmother."

"Oh, wow! Jamie, this is Alex. I haven't seen him since he was a little boy. How are you, Alex?"

"I'm fine, only my name is Alexandra now. It's great to see you. And it was nice to meet you too, Jamie," Alexandra said as she waved goodbye.

"Tell your grandmother I say hi!" said Bubbie.

"I knew Alex when he was little," Bubbie told Jamie as they walked home. "He loved to draw pictures for his grandmother and me."

"Bubbie, I think Alexandra goes by she now, not he," said Jamie.

"You're right!" said Bubbie. "I've really been putting my foot in my mouth all day, haven't I?"

"You have not!" Jamie laughed. "Can you even fit your foot in your mouth? I can't!"

"No, that's just an expression. It means I've been saying things wrong."

When they got home, Jamie's mommy joined them. Jamie said, "It's okay, Bubbie. You can't always know if someone goes by he or she or something else. Sometimes a person will tell you. If they don't, you can use the person's name or you can say they."

"That's right," Jamie's mommy added. "For example, we can say that the mail carrier is taking mail out of their mail bag and putting it in the mailbox. They are walking to the next house."

"My friend Sam goes by they," said Jamie. "They showed me their cool bike before. Remember?"

"That's true," said Jamie's mommy. "Also, sometimes people change their names or pronouns or both. So make sure you call someone by the name and pronouns they want to be called."

"It's a lot to remember, but I'll do my best.
He, she, they. His, her, their."

"You've got it! I had so much fun with you today. I love you, Bubbie!"

"I love you too, Jamie!"

Tips for Teachers, Parents, and Caregivers

Pronouns are personal—individual to each of us—and can change over time. We use pronouns when we talk about a person, and they are often tied to the person's gender. But no one has to use a gender pronoun simply because it matches the gender they were assigned at birth. Our pronouns can be an extension of our gender identity (our internal feeling of being male, female, both, or neither), but they are also about more than gender. They are a reflection and an extension of who we are in the world at this moment. It is important to always use the pronouns each person goes by because doing so:

- shows respect for and validates people

- lets people know that who they are is not based on how they look, dress, play, talk, or act

- celebrates and gives space to everyone

Using the correct pronouns people go by is equal to using the names or nicknames they request. Refusing to use someone's pronouns or assigning them different ones is harassing and offensive. It sends a message to the person, and those around them, that there is something wrong with the person. When we use the pronouns people would like us to use, we are expressing support of who they are.

A Note About the Pronouns in This Book

This book focuses on the pronouns *he, she,* and *they* (singular) since those are most commonly used, but there are many other pronouns in use. Some people choose to use *ze* and *hir* as gender-neutral pronouns, and other pronouns will be added to our language in the future.

Talking with Children About Pronouns

It's important to help children express themselves and their ideas about gender. Guiding them in sharing their pronouns is not the same as assigning them a pronoun. The more open-minded you are, the more confident children will feel in sharing their pronouns.

Creating a gender-inclusive classroom culture is key to creating an open and safe environment for children to share their pronouns. Here are a few ways to do that:

- Ask children to share their name and pronouns with the group. Start this off yourself. Say, "My name is _____ and I go by _____ pronouns." Once all children have shared, create a visual display of names and pronouns. This helps support children who are gender nonconforming.

- Use gender-neutral language for animals, insects, and inanimate objects, such as toys.

- When reading books, use a variety of pronouns to discuss the illustrations. Using the singular *they* for characters and explaining why helps children learn that they don't have to assign a female or male pronoun to everyone—it's better to use *they* than to assume someone's gender.

- Read books to the class where students can see pronouns connected to characters or real people who are transgender, gender nonconforming, agender, and so on.

Doing this helps normalize the idea that gender identity is fluid and that people don't always go by the pronouns we might assume.

- Invite someone who goes by *they / them* to talk to the class about why they chose these pronouns, and then ask children to share their pronouns.

You can also check out these resources to learn more about personal pronouns and how to use them respectfully:

- mypronouns.org
- uwm.edu/lgbtrc/qa_faqs/why-is-it-important-to-respect-peoples-pronouns
- lakeforest.edu/studentlife/intercultural/lgbtq/why-pronouns-are-important
- colorado.edu/cisc/resources/trans-queer/pronouns

Purposefully misusing pronouns can be a form of bullying. If this happens, it is important to speak to the children involved in addition to having a group discussion about using people's correct pronouns so everyone feels accepted and respected.

Ideas about gender identity are always changing and so is the related language. To best support the children and adults in our lives, it's always good to ask questions rather than assume a gendered pronoun.

....

Note: If parents or school administrators are wary of discussing gender and pronouns with young children, know that there are resources available that explain why this is an important ethical issue for the entire school community. For starters, visit naeyc.org/resources/topics and genderspectrum.org/resources.

....

THEY
THEM

About the Author and Illustrator

Afsaneh Moradian (she/her) has loved writing stories, poetry, and plays since childhood. After receiving her master's in education, she took her love of writing into the classroom where she began teaching children how to channel their creativity. Her passion for teaching has lasted for over fifteen years. Afsaneh now guides students and teachers (and her young daughter) in the art of writing. She lives in New York City and Oaxaca, Mexico.

Maria Bogade (she/her) is an illustrator and author with an animation background. She loves creating illustrations with a strong narrative, colorful and beautifully composed to entertain children and adults alike. Her work is internationally published and is also found on greeting cards and products such as chocolate. With her three children and spouse, she lives in a tiny village in southern Germany where fox and hare bid each other good night.

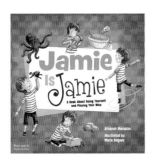

Read more about Jamie

Jamie Is Jamie
A Book About Being Yourself and Playing Your Way
by Afsaneh Moradian, illustrated by Maria Bogade
For ages 4–8. 32 pp.; HC; full-color; 8" x 8".

Other Great Books from Free Spirit

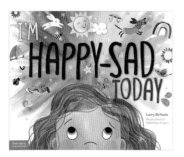

I'm Happy-Sad Today
Making Sense of
Mixed-Together Feelings
*by Lory Britain, Ph.D.,
illustrated by Matthew Rivera*

*For ages 3–8. 40 pp.; HC;
full-color; 11¼" x 9¼".*

Smarts! Everybody's Got Them
*by Thomas Armstrong, Ph.D.,
illustrated by Tim Palin*

*For ages 5–9. 44 pp.; HC;
full-color; 11¼" x 9¼".*

I'm Like You, You're Like Me
A Book About Understanding
and Appreciating Each Other
*by Cindy Gainer,
illustrated by Miki Sakamoto*

*For ages 3–8. 48 pp.; PB;
full-color; 11¼" x 9¼".*

Just Because I Am
A Child's Book of Affirmation
*by Lauren Murphy Payne, MSW,
LCSW, illustrated by Melissa Iwai*

*For ages 3–8. 36 pp.; PB and
HC; full-color; 11¼" x 9¼".*

Me and You and the Universe
*written and illustrated
by Bernardo Marçolla*

*For ages 3–8. 36 pp.;
HC w/ jacket; full-color; 8¼" x 9".*

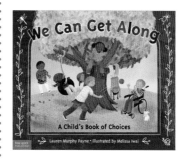

We Can Get Along
A Child's Book of Choices
*by Lauren Murphy Payne, MSW,
LCSW, illustrated by Melissa Iwai*

*For ages 3–8. 40 pp.; PB and
HC; full-color; 11¼" x 9¼".*

Interested in purchasing multiple quantities and receiving volume discounts?
Contact edsales@freespirit.com or call 1.800.735.7323 and ask for Education Sales.

Many Free Spirit authors are available for speaking engagements, workshops, and keynotes.
Contact speakers@freespirit.com or call 1.800.735.7323.

For pricing information, to place an order, or to request a free catalog, contact:

Free Spirit Publishing Inc.
6325 Sandburg Road • Suite 100 • Minneapolis, MN 55427-3674
toll-free 800.735.7323 • local 612.338.2068 • fax 612.337.5050
help4kids@freespirit.com • freespirit.com